Heidi

The Young Collector's

Illustrated Classics

Heidi

by Johanna Spyri

Adapted by
Celia Bland

Illustrated by
Eva Clift

Cover Art by Ned Butterfield

Copyright © 1996 Masterwork Books
A Division of Kidsbooks, Inc.
3535 West Peterson Avenue
Chicago, IL 60659

Manufactured in the United States of America

Contents

Chapter

①

The Alm Uncle

From the old Swiss town of Maienfeld a steep footpath winds through shady green meadows into the solemn and majestic Alps. One sunny June morning, a sturdy-looking young woman was climbing this narrow path. She led by the hand a little maiden whose cheeks glowed red as apples—and no wonder! In spite of the hot sun, she was wearing three dresses, one on top of the other, heavy boots, and a red scarf wrapped around her neck.

After an hour of climbing, the two came to the village of Dörfli, halfway up the Alm Mountain. The young woman seemed to be a native of this village, for she was greeted from every cottage, but she would not stop to talk, and put off questions with a wave of her hand.

"Wait a minute, Dete, I'll go with you," a pleasant-faced woman named Barbel called from an open doorway. The young woman stopped, and the child plopped down upon the ground.

"Are you tired, Heidi?" her companion asked.

"I'm hot," complained the little girl.

"We are almost there; just an hour farther."

Barbel joined them, and the little procession continued up the alp, the child plodding along in the rear.

"Where are you taking the little girl, Dete?" asked the newcomer. "She's your sister's child, isn't she—the orphan?"

"Yes, Barbel," Dete replied. "I am taking Heidi to live with her grandfather."

"What! To live with the Alm Uncle? Have you lost your senses?"

"He is her grandfather, and it is his turn to take care of her. I have had her till now, and I can no longer keep her."

"But you know what kind of man he is," Barbel retorted. "What will he do with a child, especially such a young one? And where are *you* going?"

"To Frankfurt," said Dete. "I have

found a good job keeping house for a wealthy family there."

"Well, I'm glad I'm not in the child's place!" Barbel muttered, with a shrug of her shoulders. "The Alm Uncle hates everyone! He never even goes to church. Tell me, Dete, what makes him look so fierce? Why does he live all alone up there on the mountain? Has he always been a hermit?"

"Well, I will tell you, but don't go gossiping it about the village," said Dete, and she glanced round to see if Heidi were so close at their heels as to hear what was said—but the little girl had disappeared!

"There she is!" cried Barbel, and pointed away from the footpath into a beautiful meadow. The little girl could be seen talking with a young boy carrying a crooked stick. "She's with Peter and his goats. He'll look after her."

"She can look after herself, that one," Dete replied. "And a good thing, too.

Her grandfather owns nothing but his hut and some goats."

"Didn't he used to have more?" Barbel asked.

"He once had the best farm on the Alm, but he was reckless and gambled everything away. He then ran away to the city and became a soldier. Some say he deserted the military after he'd killed a man in a quarrel. In any case, he came home years later with a half-grown son, Tobias, and asked his relations to take the boy in. They shut their doors in his face. He was so angry that he turned against everyone and set up a home in Dörfli with Tobias.

"When Tobias grew up, he trained as a carpenter and worked in Dörfli. He was a handsome man, well-liked by everyone, and my mother was pleased when he married my sister. But Adelheid was delicate and, when Tobias was killed by a falling beam in a house he was building, the shock killed her, too. The tragic fate of the couple was thought to be punishment for the uncle's wicked ways, which made the townspeople despise him even more. It was then that he went to live on the Alm mountaintop and never came down again. So Mother and I took Adelheid's daughter, Heidi, to live with us when she was just a year old. But now that Mother is dead and I have found this job..."

"So now you are going to leave her with that old man! I am surprised at you, Dete," Barbel said reproachfully.

"What else am I to do with her?" Dete snapped. "My job starts day after tomorrow. But where are you going, Barbel? We are already halfway up the Alm."

They had reached a hollow in the mountain, somewhat sheltered from the wind. "I have to see Peter's grandmother," said Barbel. "She spins for me in the winter. Good-bye and good luck!"

Dete watched Barbel pick her way down a stony path to a little cottage. The roof sagged and a shutter hung by one hinge. One strong winter storm, Dete thought, and the hut would be blown into the valley. She shrugged, then looked around for a glimpse of Heidi and Peter. They were nowhere in sight. Peter must have taken the goats he herded for the villagers to the meadow. Dete started up the path. Heidi had better be with him, she thought angrily.

The children had been chasing the goats, which leaped from one tasty shrub to another. At first, Heidi had panted after Peter, but the sight of the boy leaping barefoot over bush and stone gave her an idea. She sat down and pulled off her boots and stockings. Next, the three dresses were folded into a neat pile with the red scarf on top, and Heidi danced happily after Peter in just her undershirt and petticoat.

Peter grinned when he saw Heidi's new costume but said nothing—how could he when Heidi chattered nonstop, skipping beside him? How many goats did he have? Where was he taking them?

Her stream of questions was interrupted only by the sight of her Aunt Dete.

"Look at you, Heidi!" Dete scolded. "What have you done with your clothes? And where are your new boots and the stockings I knitted for you?"

The child calmly pointed down the mountain. "There," she said.

Her aunt squinted, following the direction of Heidi's finger. She could just make out the red of the scarf. "You mischievous girl! Why did you take them off?"

"I didn't need them," Heidi said, not looking in the least bit sorry.

Dete turned to Peter. "Run down and fetch them," she ordered.

"I'm already late." Peter stood with his hands in his pockets, not moving.

Dete tried another approach. "Come now, Peter," she coaxed. "You can have this new penny for your trouble."

At the sight of the shiny coin, the boy leapt into motion, taking the quickest way down the hillside. He was back so fast

that Dete could not help praising him. Peter grinned with delight as he slipped the penny into his pocket. Such treasure did not come his way very often.

Up the steep path they climbed, Heidi and the goats romping merrily in the grass. She was the first to see the old man sitting on a wooden bench outside a lonely hut, smoking a pipe. He had been watching the little group approach.

Heidi ran straight to the old man.

"How do you do, Grandfather?" she said.

"What's this?" he exclaimed. His voice was deep and gruff. He drew his bushy eyebrows together in a fierce frown as he stared at the little girl. Heidi looked into his face without once blinking her eyes.

"Good morning, Uncle," Dete called. "I have brought Tobias and Adelheid's child to live with you."

The old man glared at her, then shouted at Peter. "Here you! Get along with the goats! And take mine with you!"

Peter swung his long stick to start the goats up the mountain again. Dete continued firmly, "She's come to stay. I've done my share, Uncle. Now, it's your turn."

"Indeed!" the old man snorted, "And when the child begins to whine for you, what shall I do with her?"

"That's your business."

The look on the old man's face made Dete step back quickly. "Be off with you!" he roared. "And don't show your face here again!"

"Very well then." Dete was backing away as she spoke. "Good-bye, Heidi. Good-bye, Uncle."

Dete hurried away down the mountain to Dörfli, her conscience not quite easy about what she had done. The villagers cried to her as she passed, "Where is the child? Dete, where have you left the child?" to which she irritably replied, "Up with the Alm Uncle I tell you!"

She felt very glad that she would soon be in a fine situation, far away from the Alm Uncle and the talk of the villagers.

Chapter

At the Grandfather's

Heidi didn't notice her aunt's departure. She was too busy exploring. She peeped inside the goat shed built behind her grandfather's hut, and saw the animals' beds and feeding trough. She listened to the wind whistling and roaring through the tall fir trees that grew beside the hut. When the wind quieted she returned to her grandfather, who was blowing great clouds of smoke from his pipe and staring into the valley below. She planted herself in front of him, hands clasped behind her back.

"What do you want?" he asked gruffly.

"I want to see inside your hut."

"Come along then." Her grandfather rose and started inside. "Bring your clothes," he added.

"I don't need them anymore. I want to run around like the goats."

The old man turned around and looked sharply at Heidi. Her black eyes were shining with curiosity and excitement.

"So you shall," he said, "but bring them anyway. We'll put them in the cupboard." He added under his breath, "She's certainly not lacking in brains."

Heidi picked up the bundle and followed him into the hut's one large room. In one corner stood a bed. A table had been pushed against the far wall. Most of another wall was taken up with a fireplace in which a kettle hung bubbling over the fire.

The grandfather walked across the room and opened a door in the wall. Heidi saw three shelves. One was neatly stacked with shirts, knitted stockings, and handkerchiefs. Another held plates and cutlery, a round loaf of bread, and a slab of cheese. The lowest shelf was empty, and Heidi pushed her bundle into the darkest corner of it. She wouldn't be needing those clothes again!

"Where shall I sleep, Grandfather?" she asked.

"Wherever you like," he replied.

Heidi looked into every nook and cranny. In the corner by her grandfather's bed stood a little ladder. Climbing to its top, Heidi found herself in a loft heaped high with sweet-smelling hay. There was even a tiny window from which she could look right down into the valley!

"I'll sleep here," Heidi called to her grandfather. "It is lovely! Just come up and see how lovely it is!"

"I know all about it," sounded from below.

"I am going to make a bed," the child announced, "but you must give me a sheet."

The old man took a heavy linen sack from the cupboard and carried it up the ladder. Heidi had already shaped a bed of straw, with one end piled up higher to form a pillow. Together, she and her

grandfather tucked the heavy sheet around it. It was quite neat, and Heidi regarded it happily. "How I wish it were bedtime now!" she cried.

"I think we might have something to eat first," her grandfather remarked. "What do you say?"

"Oh yes!" Heidi cried, suddenly remembering that she had not eaten since breakfast.

"Well, let us go down, since we are agreed," said the old man, and followed close upon the child's steps. He went to the fireplace and picked up a long fork. Settling himself on a little three-legged stool, the grandfather stuck a piece of cheese on the fork and held it over the coals, turning it this way and that until it was golden brown. Heidi watched eagerly. Then she darted over to the cupboard. From the second shelf she took two plates, two knives, and a loaf of bread.

"That is right, to think of doing something yourself," said the grandfather. "But there is something still lacking."

Heidi noticed the steam coming from the kettle which hung from a hook over the fire, and she ran quickly back to the cupboard—but there was only one mug. She took the mug and a small bowl to the table.

"Very good," her grandfather said

as he settled himself on the only chair. "But where will you sit?"

Heidi picked up the three-legged stool and placed it beside the table.

"Too short," he said. "But you wouldn't be high enough in my chair either. We'll make you a table this way." The old man pushed the chair over to the stool to serve as Heidi's table. Then he poured milk into the little bowl and spread melted cheese on a round of bread. "Eat," he said, placing them on the chair seat.

Heidi grasped the bowl in both hands and drank and drank.

"I've never had such good milk in all my life," she said at last.

"Then you must have some more," the old man said, and filled her bowl again. Heidi ate her bread and toasted cheese happily, with frequent drinks of the fresh milk.

"Now we must do the chores," the grandfather said when they had finished their meal. Out in the goat shed, Heidi watched as he swept the floor clean and spread fresh straw for the goats' bed. Next, he searched in the woodpile until he found four sturdy sticks. Working away with a knife and hammer, he had soon shaped a board, made some holes in it, and put the round sticks into them.

"What is this, Heidi?" he asked.

"It's a stool," the little girl cried. "A high stool so that I can sit at the table! You made it so quickly!"

"She knows what she sees," the grandfather muttered to himself. "Her eyes are in the right place."

Evening was coming on. The wind was blowing hard in the old fir trees, whistling and moaning through the thick branches. It sounded beautiful to Heidi's ears, and she began to skip and dance. The grandfather stood in the doorway and watched her.

Suddenly, a piercing whistle rang out. Down the mountain streamed the

goats with Peter in their midst. A white goat and a brown goat bounded grace- fully out of the herd and up to the old man. In his hands he held a block of salt, which the goats eagerly began to lick.

Heidi was so full of questions she didn't know where to start. "Are they ours, Grandfather? What are their names?"

"The white goat is Little Swan, and the brown goat is Little Bear. Now, go fetch your bowl and the bread."

When Heidi came skipping back, the grandfather milked the white goat. He filled Heidi's bowl with the frothy milk, then cut a slice from the loaf.

"Here's your supper," he said. "Eat it up and then go to bed. I have to look after the goats."

The old man disappeared into the shed, the goats scampering at his heels.

"Good night, Grandfather," Heidi called. Soon she was climbing the ladder to her bed, where she slept as soundly as a princess.

Not long after, before it was entirely dark, the grandfather also went to bed. He lay listening to the wind howl among the trees. The hut trembled, and its rafters creaked. "She may be afraid," he said to himself, and climbed the ladder to the hayloft.

The moon shone brightly through the small window onto Heidi's bed. She lay sound asleep, a happy smile curved on her rosy lips. The grandfather gazed at the sweetly sleeping child for a long while. Then he went back to his own bed.

Chapter

In the Pasture

Heidi was awakened the next morning by a shrill whistle. For a moment she didn't know where she was; sunshine was pouring in her window so that the hay glistened like gold. Then she heard her grandfather's deep voice outside.

In a moment Heidi had jumped out of bed, pulled on her undershirt and petticoat, and run outside. Peter was there with his flock. Little Swan and Little Bear came tripping out of the shed in front of the grandfather.

"Would you like to go to the pasture, too?" he asked Heidi.

Heidi clapped her hands and jumped for joy.

"You must wash first." He pointed to a tub of water warming in the sun. "Come inside, General of the goats, and bring your knapsack with you."

Peter, surprised, obeyed the call and brought along the little bag which carried his meager lunch. Inside the hut, the old man cut large chunks of cheese and bread and dropped them into the boy's sack. "Now the bowl," he said as he tucked it in beside the bread. "Milk two bowls full from Little Swan for Heidi at noon. And take care that she doesn't fall off the cliffs."

"Yes, Uncle." Peter could hardly take his eyes off Heidi's bread and cheese. They were twice as big as the tiny slivers he had for his lunch.

Heidi was so delighted to be going up the mountain that she danced and skipped all the way. Bright sunshine picked out the blue and yellow of gentian and primroses in the meadows. Soon Heidi had an armful of buttercups.

The pasture where Peter usually spent the day was at the foot of a rocky mountain peak. When they reached the highest point, Peter took off his knapsack and tucked it into a hollow where it would be safe from the strong mountain winds. Heidi wrapped her flowers in her apron and tucked it in beside the knapsack. Then she sat down beside Peter and looked all around.

The valley lay far below. Before her stretched a wide field of snow—on the left, a gigantic outcropping of rock and bald jagged cliffs rose sternly into the blue sky. Everywhere there was a deep stillness. Peter, who had been up before dawn gathering his herd from the villagers, lay down and closed his eyes.

Heidi played quietly with the goats until Peter woke up from his nap and began setting out their meal. He spread a square of cloth on the grass. On one side he put Heidi's large pieces of bread and cheese, on the other, his small ones. Then he called Little Swan and milked her.

"Where do you get *your* milk?" she asked him.

"From Snail, my goat," Peter replied pointing to a skinny little animal.

Heidi drank two bowls of milk, then ate some bread. The cheese she handed to Peter.

"You may have that," she said. "I've had enough."

Peter stared at her in surprise. When he did not take the food from her hand, she lay it on his knee. Still puzzled, the goatherd bobbed his head in thanks, then ate the largest meal he'd ever had in his life.

Peter was licking the last crumbs from his fingers when he suddenly turned his head and listened intently. Jumping up, he began to run.

"What is it, Peter?" Heidi cried. She ran after him to the cliff's edge, where a little goat was leaping heedlessly. Peter flung himself down on the ground and just managed to seize one of its legs before it fell into the ravine to a certain death. The goat bleated in fear and struggled to free itself from Peter's grasp.

"Help me, Heidi," Peter cried.

Heidi pulled a handful of sweet-smelling herbs from the earth and held them under the goat's nose. "Come, little goat, be good," she coaxed. "You don't want to fall and break your bones, do you?"

The goat stopped thrashing and turned to nibble on the herbs. Peter seized its collar and hoisted it back onto safe ground.

"There!" he cried, and lifted his long stick to beat the little animal.

"No, no!" Heidi protested. She grabbed his arm, her eyes flashing. "I won't let you!"

"He can go," Peter said slyly, "if you promise to give me some of your cheese again tomorrow."

Heidi readily agreed. "You can have it all. Tomorrow and every day. But you must promise not to hit the goats—not this one or any one."

Peter shrugged. "It's all the same to me," he said. He let go of the goat, and it bounded back to the flock.

The day passed quickly. As the sun began to sink behind the great peak of the mountain, the snow reflected its light in a glory of rose and gold. Heidi let out a scream. "Peter! The mountain! It's on fire!"

"It is always so when evening comes," Peter explained. "It's not really on fire."

"But what is it? Look at the snow and those tall pointy rocks. What are they called?"

"Mountains don't have names," he said.

"Oh look! The fire has gone out! Everything is grey." Heidi sank sadly to the ground beside Peter, who was peeling the bark off a new staff.

"It will be just the same tomorrow," he said. "Get up! We must go home."

When they reached the hut, Heidi ran straight to her grandfather. "It was so beautiful," she cried. "The fire on the mountain and the snow and the flowers.

See what I've brought you!" She shook
out her apron, but the flowers that
tumbled to the ground were not the
ones she had picked. Instead, they
looked like wisps of hay.

"What's happened?" Heidi cried.

"Flowers like to stand out in the sunshine rather than be shut up in your apron," the grandfather explained.

"Then I will never pick them again. Grandfather, why don't the mountains have names? And why does the fire come at night?"

"Jump into the washtub while I milk the goats," the old man said, "and then I'll tell you."

Over their supper of milk and bread, her grandfather explained, "The mountains do have names. The one you were on is called Falcon's Nest. Did you like it there?"

"Oh, yes!" the child exclaimed. "Especially when the fire came. Why did that happen?"

The grandfather stroked his beard thoughtfully. "You see, that is the sun's way of saying good night to the mountains. The sun sends them its most beautiful rays so that they may not forget it before the next morning."

This pleased Heidi, and she could hardly wait for another day to see the sun again. But first she had to go to sleep, and that night she dreamed of goats leaping up the steep slopes of a shining mountain.

Chapter

At the Grandmother's

As the summer passed, Heidi grew very tanned and strong and healthy, and she was as happy as the merry little birds in the trees. Soon came the autumn, and one frosty morning Peter arrived blowing on his fingers to keep them warm. Heidi prepared to go with him to the meadow but her grandfather said, "Not today, Heidi. That strong wind might blow you right over the cliffs."

So, as the days grew shorter and the snows came, Heidi spent much of her time sitting on her stool near the fire watching her grandfather make pretty round goat cheeses or work with his hammer and nails at his carpenter's bench. One afternoon, as Heidi and her grandfather were sitting at the table having lunch, they heard a great stamping sound outside the hut. Finally, the door flew open and Peter burst in. Snow clung to his hair, covered his jacket, and sat in clumps on his boots.

Heidi laughed at the sight of him, for as he warmed himself by the fire, the snow that covered his clothes began to melt. She thought he looked like a waterfall.

"How are you, General?" the grandfather asked. "I suppose that since you no longer have a goat army, you must chew on your pencil instead?"

Heidi was instantly curious. "Why must he do that?"

"Sometimes chewing a pencil helps with difficult tasks like reading and writing," the grandfather explained. "Isn't that right, General?"

Heidi was fascinated by this bit of information, and she peppered Peter with questions about school.

Finally, the old man said, "Well, General, now you have been under fire and need strengthening. Come, stay to supper with us."

Peter's eyes widened when he saw what a fine piece of sausage the Alm

Uncle had placed on his plate alongside a thick slice of bread. Peter had not eaten anything so good for ages, and he ate with relish.

After their meal, Peter started for home. "I'm in school all week," he told Heidi as he stood in the doorway, "but I'll try to come again next Sunday; and you must come visit my grandmother some-time."

The idea delighted Heidi. "We must go see Peter's grandmother today," she said the next morning, and the next. "She is expecting us." But each time, the old man replied, "Not today, the snow is too deep."

On the fourth day, when the cold was so bitter that the snow cracked with every footstep, Heidi said again, "Today I really must go to the grandmother's. She will tire of waiting for me."

The grandfather rose from the table, went up to the hayloft, and brought down Heidi's heavy coverlet. "Well, come along!" he said.

Heidi threw on her warmest clothes and ran outside to find her grandfather sitting on a large sled. He placed Heidi in front of him and wrapped her in the coverlet. Holding her tightly with one arm, he took hold of a large stick attached to a steering bar across the front of the sled, gave a mighty push with his feet, and they were off. Straight down the mountain they flew, with a spray of snow from the runners streaming into their faces. They stopped right in front of Peter's hut.

The old man helped Heidi out of the sled and said, "You go inside, and when it begins to grow dark, come out again and start up the mountain."

Then he turned around with his sled and began pulling it up the snowy path.

Heidi opened the door of the rickety hut and stepped inside. By the glow of a small fireplace she could see a little old woman bent over a spinning wheel.

"How do you do, Grandmother?"

The old woman lifted her head and sought with her hand until she touched the hand Heidi held out to her. "Are you the child who is living with the Alm Uncle?" she asked.

"Yes. I'm Heidi."

"How does the child look, Brigitte?" she called to Peter's mother. "Is she frail like her mother, Adelheid?"

"She has curly hair like Tobias, and a delicate form like her mother. She looks very well."

"So what Peter says must be true. The Alm Uncle is taking good care of her. Who ever would have believed such a thing!"

As the women talked over her head, Heidi gazed around. She saw the shutters sagging on their hinges and said suddenly, "My grandfather will mend those for you. He can fix anything."

"Oh, you good child!" cried the grandmother. "I fear you are mistaken."

"No, no, Grandmother, he will mend it for you. Then the light will come in the window, and you will be able to see."

"Ah, child, I can see nothing, nothing at all."

"But in summer, when the sun sets the mountains on fire, then you'll be able to see, won't you?"

"No, child. I will never see again."

Heidi burst into tears. "Can't anyone make you see?" she cried.

"Come here, Heidi, and sit with me," the old woman said gently. "When a person is blind, it's good to hear a friendly voice. Tell me what you and the Alm Uncle do up on the mountain."

Heidi dried her tears, and began telling the old woman about the two goats and how her grandfather brushed and combed them, and how she was learning to feed them.

Suddenly there was a great stamping of feet and Peter burst into the room.

"What, home from school already?"

the grandmother cried. "How quickly the day has flown by! How are you, Peter? How did you get along with the reading?"

Peter shrugged and grinned. "Oh, the same."

"Peter, Peter," the old woman sighed. "You'll be twelve in February and still you can't read!"

"Why does that matter?" Heidi asked.

"Look up on that shelf, child. Do you see an old book? It's full of beautiful hymns. I want so much to hear them again, but reading is too difficult for Peter." She sighed.

"He'll learn someday, Mother," Brigitte said. "Fetch a lamp, Peter. It's getting dark."

"Oh," cried Heidi. "I must go!" She pulled on her coat and ran to kiss the old woman's cheek.

"Don't go alone!" the grandmother said. "Go with her, Peter." But Heidi slipped out the door before anyone could move.

"Go after her, Brigitte, run! She will freeze!" commanded Peter's grandmother.

Brigitte obeyed, but she had gone only a few steps before she saw the grandfather coming down the snowy mountain.

"Very good, Heidi," the old man said. "You have kept your word." He wrapped the coverlet around the girl, took her in his arms, and began climbing back up the mountain. Brigitte saw this and went back into the hut and told the grandmother all about it.

"God be praised," cried the old woman. "He is so good to her!"

At supper that night, Heidi declared to the grandfather, "Tomorrow you must take your hammer and nails down to Peter's house and mend the shutters."

"Who says I must?" her grandfather demanded gruffly.

"I do! The grandmother is afraid of the noise when the shutters bang. She fears that the roof will tumble down on their heads. Can we go and help her tomorrow?"

Heidi had come to stand beside the old man and he looked long into her eager little face. "Tomorrow," he promised.

The next afternoon, Heidi and her grandfather again swooped down the mountainside on the sled. "Go in," the old man urged once they were at Peter's hut. "And when it is dark, come back outside."

Heidi opened the door and the grandmother called out joyfully from her corner, "Here is the child!"

Scarcely had Heidi pushed a low stool near the old woman's spinning wheel than a great pounding sound could be heard outside the house. The noise startled the grandmother so much that she jumped up, nearly upsetting the spinning wheel. "It is happening!" she cried. "The hut is tumbling to pieces!"

"Don't be afraid," Heidi said, taking the old woman by the arm. "It's only Grandfather. He is mending everything."

"Brigitte," the grandmother called. "Go and see! Is it really the Alm Uncle?"

Brigitte found the old man nailing down a loose shingle. "Good day, Uncle," she said, nervously. "Mother and I are very grateful—"

"Enough!" the grandfather snapped. "I know too well what you and the villagers think of me. Go back in the house. I can see for myself what needs to be done."

Brigitte hurried inside again, and

reported their conversation to the grandmother. "You see, God has not forgotten us," the old woman replied.

And so the winter passed. Every day the grandfather wrapped Heidi in the coverlet for the ride down the mountain. Every day he stopped up more holes and nailed down more boards until the grandmother's hut was snug and sound.

Heidi was sad when she realized that not even her grandfather could make the old woman see again, but the grandmother reassured her. "Your voice helps me to see," she said. "Tell me again about your days up on the mountain with the goats.

Chapter

5

A Visitor

Two winters passed, and Heidi was as happy as the birds in the air. Then, in the spring, a visitor arrived. Just as Heidi and her grandfather were clearing the table, Aunt Dete swept into the hut wearing a fine hat with a feather, and a skirt so long it dragged the floor.

"How well you look, Heidi!" she exclaimed nervously. "I knew the air up here would be good for you."

Heidi looked at her grandfather. He was frowning, his pipe clenched so tightly between his teeth that it looked as if he wanted to bite it in half. Still, he said nothing as Dete chattered on.

"I knew Heidi would be in your way, Uncle, so I have found a wonderful home for her in Frankfurt with a wealthy family. Heidi will be a playmate for a little girl who is confined to a wheelchair. She will be treated just like one of the family rather than a servant. She will eat at the same table, study with the girl's tutor—who knows what might come of it?"

"Have you finished?" the grandfather snapped.

"Bah," snorted Dete with a toss of her head. "You act as if opportunities such as this come along every day. Heidi is eight years old now, and she can't even read. What kind of future is she going to have living up here with you?"

"Silence!" roared the Alm Uncle, his eyes blazing. "Take her and be gone!" He stormed out of the hut.

"You have made my grandfather angry," said Heidi, frowning.

"He will get over it soon. Now come," urged Dete, "where are your clothes?"

"I will not come," Heidi said.

"What?" Dete snapped. "Don't be foolish and stubborn like the goats. Your grandfather wants you to come with me. You heard him. You can't imagine what a good time you'll have." She went to the cupboard and packed Heidi's things.

"Here is your hat," she continued. "Put it on. If you don't like it in Frankfurt, you can come back."

"Tonight?"

"Yes, yes, now come along." Aunt Dete put the bundle of clothes under her arm, took Heidi by the hand, and they started down the mountain.

"Peter's grandmother!" Heidi cried

as they came to the mountain hollow. "I must say good-bye to her."

"No time for that," Dete insisted. "We'll find a nice gift for her in Frankfurt. Some soft white rolls, perhaps. I imagine she can hardly eat black bread any longer."

"Oh, yes!" Heidi agreed, and she began pulling at her aunt's hand. So it was that as they reached Dörfli, the villagers saw Heidi running ahead of her aunt.

"You see how it is," Dete called to the villagers. "The child is in a hurry."

"She can hardly wait to get away from that terrible old man," the villagers whispered to each other.

From that day on, the grandfather looked more ferocious than ever. Only Peter's old blind grandmother stood by the Alm Uncle, and she told everyone who came to her house to bring spinning or to get yarn, how kind he had been to Heidi, and how he had repaired their

hut, but no one believed her stories. The grandmother herself saw no more of the Alm Uncle, and her days were once again empty. "Ah!" she would sigh, "if only I could hear Heidi's voice once more before I die."

Chapter 6

In Frankfurt

"Is it time yet, Fräulein Rottenmeier?" asked the thin little girl for the second time. The housekeeper did not raise her eyes from her embroidery. "Be patient, Miss Klara," she said.

Klara's mother had died many years before, and Herr Sesemann, Klara's father, was often away on business, so the housekeeper Fräulein Rottenmeier was in charge of everything in the Sesemann

household. She had a solemn expression and wore a short cape over her shoulders and a large cap perched on her head. "They will be here soon," she said decidedly.

Just then the doorbell rang, and a rather sour-faced maid announced that there were visitors. Fräulein Rottenmeier rose slowly from her chair as Heidi and her Aunt Dete entered the room.

"So this is the child," Fräulein Rottenmeier said in an unfriendly voice as she examined the newcomer. "That is a disgraceful hat she is wearing. What is your name, child?"

"Heidi."

"What? How odd! That cannot be your real name. What name were you given at birth?"

"I don't know," replied the girl.

"What an answer!" the housekeeper exclaimed. "Dete, is she foolish or pert?"

"If you please, Fräulein," Dete said, as she curtsied to the housekeeper. "She was named after my sister Adelheid."

"Well! Adelheid is a name that can at least be pronounced. How old is she?"

"Ten years old," Dete replied.

"My grandfather says that I am eight," Heidi insisted.

"Only eight years old!" the house-keeper exclaimed. "Klara is twelve. I informed you, Dete, that Klara's companion must be of her own age. What books have you studied, child?"

"None," Heidi answered.

"What? How did you ever learn to read?"

"I have never learned."

"Good gracious! You cannot read! Dete, this is not part of the agreement. How could you bring me this creature?"

"If you remember, Fräulein," Dete said calmly, "you asked for an unspoiled child. This one fills the bill exactly. Now, if you will excuse me, my mistress is expecting me." Dete curtsied again and was out the door before the other woman could respond.

"Wait!" Fräulein Rottenmeier called angrily, and she rushed after her.

Heidi stood where her aunt had left her and began to examine the room. Until now, Klara had watched in silence. Now she beckoned to Heidi and said, "Come here."

Heidi turned at the sound of the soft voice and saw a girl with gentle eyes sitting in a wheelchair by a small table.

"Shall I call you Heidi or Adelheid?" the girl asked.

"My name is Heidi."

"Then I shall call you that. My name is Klara. Did you want to come to Frankfurt?"

"No," Heidi responded. "Tomorrow I am going back home again to bring the grandmother some white rolls."

"You are a strange child!" Klara exclaimed. "Don't you know that they have brought you here to keep me company?"

Fräulein Rottenmeier came bustling back into the room. "That tiresome Dete was gone before I could get downstairs. We shall have to make the best of it."

She clapped her hands sharply and called, "Tinette? Sebastian?" The double doors at the back of the room swung open.

"Tinette, make a room ready for the young miss." The maid threw a disdainful look at Heidi, then flounced off. The housekeeper next addressed Sebastian, the butler. "We shall have dinner now. Take Miss Klara in."

Heidi could not take her eyes off Sebastian. She placed herself in front of him and announced, "You look just like Peter, the goatherd!"

The housekeeper clasped her hands in horror. "Don't ever address servants in that familiar way! Clearly, I shall have to teach you manners."

Sebastian placed Klara at the table. The housekeeper sat next to Klara and beckoned Heidi to take the place opposite. Next to Heidi's plate was a fine white roll. When Sebastian offered her fish from a large tray, she pointed to the roll and said, "Can I have that?"

Sebastian nodded. In a twinkling, Heidi slipped it into her apron pocket. Sebastian made a face to keep from laughing. He remained standing silently by Heidi, for he did not dare to speak, or to move away until he was bidden.

"Shall I eat some of that?" the girl asked, pointing to the fish.

Sebastian nodded again.

"Then give me some."

Shocked at Heidi's brash manners, Fräulein Rottenmeier quickly reprimanded the child. Sebastian tried to hide his amusement but, in doing so, the tray in his hand began to tremble.

"You may go now, Sebastian," the housekeeper ordered. "Put the tray down."

All through dinner, Fräulein Rottenmeier lectured Heidi on how she was to behave in a gentleman's house, but the little girl was so tired from her long journey she scarcely heard a word.

When Sebastian came to clear the plates, he found Heidi fast asleep in her chair. She didn't wake even when he carried her upstairs to the little corner room Tinette had prepared for her.

When Heidi awoke the next morning, everything was strange to her: the high white bed, the washstand, the long curtain covering the closed window. Longing for fresh air, she tried but could not get the window to open. She dressed herself slowly and went downstairs to find Klara.

Out in the hall Fräulein Rottenmeier was speaking to the schoolmaster. "A word, Herr Kandidat," she said. "We have a young visitor from the Swiss Alps. She will be a companion for Klara and will be treated as one of the family. I must warn you however that she does not even know her alphabet."

"I do not mind teaching her the alphabet, Fräulein," the tutor responded.

"Good. But if the child holds Miss Klara back in any way you must inform Herr Sesemann."

The tutor bowed politely. He had just turned to enter the library when he heard a loud crash. Fräulein Rottenmeier swept past him and flung open the door.

A small table lay on its side, books and papers were strewn everywhere, and they glimpsed Heidi running out the other door.

"That wretched child! What has she done now?" Fräulein Rottenmeier cried.

"It was an accident," Klara gasped between gales of laughter. "She heard the carriages in the street and ran to look at them."

"You see how it is, Herr Kandidat. She has no idea of how to behave in polite society," the housekeeper rejoined. She hurried downstairs to find Heidi standing in the open doorway looking puzzled.

"I thought I heard the wind in the fir trees. But I can't see them anywhere," Heidi told the housekeeper sadly.

"Firs? Do you think we live in a forest? Come upstairs immediately and let us have no more of this wild running about. Do you understand, Adelheid?"

Heidi sighed. "Yes, Fräulein."

By the time Sebastian had cleaned

up the mess in the library, there was no time left for lessons. Because she was not well Klara napped in the afternoons; Heidi was instructed to do as she liked, so long as she stayed out of mischief.

Heidi sat herself down on the stairs and waited for Sebastian. "Excuse me," she said when he appeared carrying a tray.

"Yes?" he said crossly.

Heidi hesitated, then asked, "How do you open the window?"

"Is that all?" Sebastian laughed and, leading the little girl into the dining room, he swung open one large window. With a joyful cry, Heidi ran to look outside.

"But there is only the stony street!" she cried. "Where do you go to see the whole valley?"

Sebastian scratched his head. "Well, I supposed you would have to go up in that church tower over there. The one with the golden dome."

"Thank you, Sebastian," Heidi said. Straight away, she ran down the stairs and out the front door.

Chapter

7

Fräulein Rottenmeier's Uncomfortable Day

Out on the street, Heidi didn't know which way to turn. The tower that had seemed so close when she was looking out the window was nowhere to be seen. She ran down the length of the street until she came to another street and then another. A great many people passed her, but they were all in such a hurry that Heidi could not ask them for directions. Finally, she noticed a boy standing on the corner; he was carrying a small hand organ on his back and a very strange animal in his arms.

"Where is the tower with the golden dome?" she asked him.

"Don't know," was his answer.

"Don't you know of any church with a high tower?"

"Certainly I do, but what will you give me to show you where it is?" the boy inquired.

"What do you want?" Heidi asked.

The boy held out his hand. Heidi searched her pocket. She pulled out a little picture on which was painted a garland of red roses. She looked at it for a little while, for she hated to part with it; Klara had painted it for her that morning. But to look down into the valley, and across the green slopes!

"Here," she said, holding out the picture to him, "will you take this?"

The boy laughed in a mean sort of way. "I want four pennies," he said.

"I haven't any money," Heidi said, "but Klara has, and she will give you some."

"Come along then," the boy said, and the two started off down the street. They had not gone far before Heidi was asking him all about the organ on his back. He showed her how he turned the handle to play music and how his companion, a trained monkey, danced.

Before Heidi could ask any more

questions they had reached the church. Its heavy wooden door was closed.

"How do we get in?" she asked.

"Don't know."

"Perhaps I could ring the bell as I ring for Sebastian." Heidi rang the doorbell and from a long way away she heard a faint clanging.

"You must wait here while I go up," Heidi said, "and then show me the way back."

"You must give me another four pennies," the boy said.

Just then the door creaked open and an old man peered out. "Be off with you," he barked.

"But I want to go to the tower," Heidi said.

"Go home," the caretaker snapped. "And don't ring my bell again or I'll call the constable."

"Please," Heidi pleaded. "Just once."

"Oh, very well," he grumbled. "Come along then."

Taking Heidi's hand, he led her inside. "You stay there," he said to the boy and slammed the door.

They climbed and climbed. The dark staircase grew narrower and the steps smaller until finally they saw light above them and they were on a platform surrounded by high walls. In each wall was a large window. The old man lifted Heidi so she could look out, but all she saw was a sea of roofs and towers and chimneys.

"Oh," she exclaimed, disappointed. "It's not at all what I had hoped for."

"What would a child like you know about views?" sniffed her companion. "Well, you've had your look. Come down. And mind you leave my doorbell alone after this."

Halfway down, the staircase widened out to a landing where the caretaker had his room. Beside his door was a basket in which lay a large grey cat. She meowed warningly when Heidi came near, but the old man said, "Come, you may look at the kittens. She won't hurt you while I'm here."

Heidi went toward the basket and shrieked with delight. "Oh, the lovely little creatures!"

"Would you like one?" asked the tower-keeper.

"For my own?"

"Yes. You can have them all if you like," he added slyly. "I will bring them to you, only tell me where."

Heidi was filled with joy. How surprised and pleased Klara would be when the kittens arrived! "To Herr Sesemann's big house. There is a golden head of a dog with a big ring in his mouth on the front door. Can I carry one or two with me—one for myself and one for Klara?"

"Well, wait a little," said the keeper; and he carried the old cat into his room, put her into the cupboard, shut the door, and came back. "There now, take two!"

Heidi chose a white kitten and a striped yellow-and-white one, and put one in her right pocket and one in her left. Then she went down the stairs.

The boy was still sitting on the steps outside, and when the keeper had closed the door, Heidi said, "Which is the way to Herr Sesemann's house?"

"Don't know," the boy replied.

"The roof of the house goes like this," Heidi explained, making a steeple with her fingers.

The boy jumped up. All he needed was a clue like this to be able to find the way. He started off on the run and Heidi after him, and in a short time they stood in front of the door with the big brass knocker. Heidi rang the bell and Sebastian answered.

"Quick! Quick!" he exclaimed when he saw Heidi.

Heidi ran inside and Sebastian closed the door on the boy.

"Quick!" urged Sebastian, "Go right to the dining room. Fräulein Rottenmeier looks like a loaded cannon."

The housekeeper stared stonily at Heidi as she came into the room. Klara sat with her eyes on her plate. There was an uncomfortable silence.

"Adelheid," Fräulein Rottenmeier began, "I have only this to say. You have behaved very badly, and really deserve to be punished for leaving the house without asking permission—"

"Meow."

"What did you say? How dare you mock me?"

"But I didn't—" Heidi exclaimed.

"Meow, meow!"

Sebastian rushed from the room.

"Heidi," Klara gasped. "Why do you keep doing that? You can see how angry—"

Almost in tears, Heidi burst out, "It's the kittens!"

"What? Kittens!" screamed Fräulein Rottenmeier. "Sebastian! Find the horrible creatures and take them away!"

The housekeeper rushed from the room. Sebastian, his hand over his mouth to hide his laughter, returned to find Klara holding the kittens in her lap, and Heidi kneeling by her side, playing with the two graceful creatures.

"Sebastian," Klara pleaded, "you must find a bed for the kittens where Fräulein Rottenmeier will not see them."

"I'll take care of them, Miss Klara," the butler promised. "A nice little basket where the Fräulein won't find them."

On the following morning, Sebastian had no sooner shown Herr Kandidat to the library, than the doorbell rang with such force, Sebastian was certain it was Herr Sesemann, himself. To his surprise, he found a ragged boy with a hand organ standing on the steps.

"What do you mean by ringing this bell? Be off with you!"

"I want to see Klara," the boy insisted.

"How does a dirty street urchin like you know Miss Klara?"

"I showed her the way home yesterday."

A sly smile lit Sebastian's face. He knew Heidi must be up to some mischief again. "Well, well," he said. "Come in. You may play your music box for Miss Klara. She'll like that. Follow me."

Sebastian knocked on the library door, then opened it. "A boy to see Miss Klara," he announced.

"May he come in, Herr Kandidat?" Klara asked, but the boy was already in the room. Straight away he began playing his organ.

Klara and Heidi were enchanted. They clapped their hands and asked him to play again. Herr Kandidat kept clearing his throat as if he were about to say something, but he didn't. Suddenly, Fräulein Rottenmeier rushed into the room.

"What's going on here? Who is this? Sebastian, take him away at once!"

The butler quickly hurried the boy out of the library and down the stairs.

"Here you are," he said at the front door. "Eight pennies for seeing the young miss home and eight more for the music."

But the morning's surprises were far from over. No sooner had Herr Kandidat settled his students back to work, than the doorbell rang again. It was a man carrying a large covered basket for Miss Klara!

"For me? Let me see!" the girl cried when Sebastian brought it to the library.

"Perhaps it would be better to wait until after the lesson," Herr Kandidat suggested.

But it was too late. As soon as Sebastian set the basket down, the cover popped open and one, two, three kittens jumped out and began to scamper around the room so fast it seemed as if the whole room were full of the tiny creatures. Heidi scooped up two and ran after the third, as even more kittens escaped from under the wicker lid.

"There!" Klara cried, pointing under the table. "And there!"

"Young ladies, young ladies!" the tutor protested, but neither child paid any attention to him—they were too busy chasing the cunning creatures. With Sebastian's help, the kittens had all been returned to the basket when Fräulein Rottenmeier appeared.

"What is happening here? Adelheid, get up off the floor." The housekeeper was so busy scolding Heidi that she didn't notice Sebastian whisk the basket out of the room.

"What is to be done with you, Adelheid? You have no sense of how to behave. I know of only one punishment that will have any effect on you, for you are sassy and undisciplined. You will spend the rest of the day in the cellar with the lizards and rats."

Heidi listened wonderingly, for she had never been in a frightful cellar; the cellar in her grandfather's hut was a pleasant place where milk and cheeses were kept. But Herr Kandidat looked shocked and Klara gasped, "No, Fräulein Rottenmeier! You must wait until Papa returns. He has already written that he is coming soon. Let him decide."

The housekeeper frowned and swept out the room.

Soon afterwards, Sebastian returned to the library. In a whisper, he informed Klara that he had hidden all the kittens in the attic. When Fräulein Rottenmeier was out of the house, he promised, he would spirit them into Klara's room for the girls to play with.

That evening, Heidi told Klara stories about Peter and the goats and the great fir trees, until her longing for the Alm became so great she cried out,"I really must go home now! Tomorrow I really must go!"

But Klara quieted her, reminding Heidi that she must surely remain until her papa came home. Then, they would see what would happen.

In the meantime, Heidi tried to learn how to read, but no matter how patient Herr Kandidat was, she did not seem to be able to sort out one letter from another. As the days passed, the tutor noticed that Heidi became quieter and quieter. Sebastian noted that she sat still as a mouse at the table and did not stir; but she always put her bread quickly into her pocket.

Only the slowly growing pile of white rolls, hidden in a shawl at the bottom of her closet, comforted her. At least, when she went home, she would have a wonderful present to give to Peter's grandmother.

Chapter

The Master of the House

As the day of Herr Sesemann's expected arrival approached, Fräulein Rottenmeier determined to improve Heidi's wardrobe with some of Klara's hand-me-down clothing. The housekeeper went to Heidi's closet to examine the things she already had, and to decide what should be kept and what disposed of. But a few moments later she came into the library looking very disgusted.

"What a discovery I have made, Adelheid!" she exclaimed. "In your clothes closet, what do I find? A pile of rolls tied up in a shawl!"

"Tinette!" she then called into the dining room, "take away the old bread in Adelheid's closet and that crushed straw hat on the bed table."

"No! No!" screamed Heidi. "I must have the hat, and the rolls are for the grandmother!" Heidi was about to rush after Tinette but the housekeeper held her back. Heidi threw herself down by Klara's chair and began to cry in despair, "Now the grandmother won't have any rolls. They were for the grandmother; now she won't have any!"

"Heidi, please don't cry," Klara begged. "You shall have as many rolls as you wish. I promise."

"As many as I had saved up?"

"Even more! And they'll be soft, fresh ones. Those had gone hard. They wouldn't have been any good."

Although Klara's promise comforted Heidi, she still had red eyes when she appeared at the dinner table. Sebastian kept making the most meaningful gestures whenever he came near Heidi. He would wink as if to make her understand: "Be comforted! I have looked out for everything and made it all right."

A little later, when Heidi went to her room and was about to get into bed, she found her little crumpled straw hat hidden under the bedspread. Tenderly, Heidi smoothed out its bent brim and tucked it away in the back of her closet.

A few days later, Heidi and Klara were sitting in Klara's room looking at a picture book when they heard carriage wheels clattering on the cobblestones outside. A few minutes later, Herr Sesemann walked into the room.

"Papa!" Klara cried, holding out her

arms. Heidi walked to the far side of the room and waited quietly while father and daughter kissed. Then Herr Sesemann turned and held out his hand to Heidi. "And this is our little Swiss girl. Are you happy here, my dear? Are you and Klara good friends?"

"Klara is always good to me," Heidi replied.

"Heidi makes me very happy, Papa," Klara said quickly.

"I'm glad to hear it. Now I must have some lunch. I'll be back to talk after I've eaten."

In the dining room, Fräulein Rottenmeier was waiting with a sour look on her face.

"I am sorry to report, Herr Sesemann, that our little visitor has filled the house with strange people and animals in your absence; the creature's conduct is past understanding. I am afraid she may be out of her mind!"

"Good heavens! And yet Klara seemed very lively."

Herr Sesemann looked at the housekeeper very closely, as if he wanted to assure himself that the matter was truly serious and not the product of the woman's imagination. "Pray excuse me," he said. "I must speak to Klara about this matter."

In the library he found the two friends chatting and giggling. Herr Sesemann turned toward Heidi and said, "Look here, bring me—" Herr Sesemann did not exactly know what he wanted, but he wished to send Heidi away for a little while. "Bring me a glass of water, please," he said.

Heidi disappeared.

"Now, my dear Klara," said her papa, "Do you want me to send Heidi away?"

"No, no, Papa! Don't do that!" Klara begged. "We have so much fun and time goes so quickly now that she is here!"

"Very good, Klara; and here comes your little friend back again. Thank you, child. Now I have a surprise for you both. I must go back to Paris next week, but Grandmamma will be coming for a nice long visit."

Before Herr Sesemann left, he informed the housekeeper that Heidi was to be treated kindly, and that if she could not deal with the child alone, that Frau Sesemann, his mother, would certainly manage.

A week later, when a carriage stopped at the front door, Fräulein Rottenmeier sent Heidi up to her room. "Frau Sesemann will want to see Klara first," she explained. But moments later, the maid Tinette rapped at Heidi's door. "Go into the library," she said in her sharp way.

Klara's grandmother was sitting in a low chair with her feet on a little stool. Heidi went to her and took the soft white hand that was held out to her. Frau Sesemann had lovely white hair crowned by a lacy white cap.

"What is your name, child?" she asked.

"My name is Heidi; but if I must be called Adelheid, I'll answer to that."

"Frau Sesemann will doubtless admit," broke in Fräulein Rottenmeier, "that I had to choose a name which

could be pronounced without so much difficulty by the servants."

"My dear Rottenmeier," replied Frau Sesemann, "if a person is named Heidi, I will call her so. Now please fetch the parcel on my bed. I have brought some books for *Heidi.*"

The housekeeper sniffed. "Books will do her no good. She does not even know her alphabet. If Herr Kandidat did not possess the patience of an angel from heaven, he would long ago have given up trying to teach her."

As the housekeeper left the room, Frau Sesemann asked, "Is this true, Heidi? Can't you read?"

Heidi sighed. "No, Madam. Peter says reading is too difficult, so I knew I wouldn't be able to."

"Firstly, this Peter sounds like a very strange person. And secondly, you must call me Grandmamma. Never mind, we will soon have you reading."

From that day on, while Klara was resting, Heidi spent every afternoon in the library with Frau Sesemann looking through beautiful story books. One day she found a picture of a green meadow. Two frisky goats frolicked beside a boy who stood leaning on his stick. Suddenly, tears flowed down the little girl's cheeks.

"What is it, child?," asked the grandmamma worriedly. "Don't cry. The picture made you remember something?

As soon as you have learned to read you shall have that book for your own, and you will learn the whole story of the shepherd and his goats. You would like that wouldn't you, Heidi?"

Heidi nodded, still sobbing. She felt she could not tell the grandmamma how she longed for the mountains and her grandfather. Fräulein Rottenmeier had warned her that Klara and Herr Sesemann would think her ungrateful if she complained and asked to go home.

"My dear, I've noticed that you seem unhappy sometimes," the grandmamma said. "If you cannot tell anyone what your trouble is, it is a good idea to ask God for help."

"I'll pray tonight," Heidi promised. She would ask God to send her home to the Alm, she decided.

Chapter

9

The Ghost

The grandmamma's visit was almost over when Herr Kandidat came to her one day. "The most unusual occurrence has arisen," he began. "I had almost given up hope—"

"Are you trying to tell me," Frau Sesemann interrupted, "that Heidi has learned to read?"

The tutor stared in surprise. "Yes, indeed!"

Frau Sesemann just smiled, and that day at the dinner table Heidi found her favorite story book at her place.

"Is it for me?" she asked. "To keep forever?"

"Forever," said the grandmamma.

"Even when I go home?"

"But you won't go home for a long time, will you Heidi?" Klara interrupted. "I would miss you so much!"

Heidi sighed and said nothing, but she hugged the book to her chest and slept with it under her pillow that night.

Finally, the day for the grandmamma's departure arrived, and Heidi grew even more forlorn. The house seemed as still as if everything had come to an end, and throughout the rest of the day, Klara and Heidi sat dejectedly, and did not know what to do with themselves.

When their lessons were over, Heidi announced, "I am going to read aloud to you, Klara, from the book Grandmamma gave me."

However, it was not long after Heidi began her task that it all came to an end. She had scarcely begun to read a story about a dying grandmother when she suddenly screamed aloud, "Oh, the grandmother is dead!" and burst into pitiful weeping.

"Now the grandmother is dead and I can never go to her, and she has never had a single roll!" she cried.

Klara tried to explain to Heidi that it was not the grandmother on the Alm, only one in a story who had died, but the girl could not calm herself.

Meanwhile, Fräulein Rottenmeier had come into the room and heard Klara's attempt to explain Heidi's mistake. When the child continued sobbing, she said impatiently, "Adelheid, we have had enough of this screaming. If you ever again give vent to such behavior I will take your book away from you."

Heidi turned pale with fright. The book was her treasure. She hastily dried her tears and did not cry again, no matter what she read. Instead, she saved her tears for her pillow, weeping for hours every night before falling asleep.

Winter slowly became spring, and Heidi grew pale and thin with the effort of holding her homesickness inside.

Fräulein Rottenmeier was also having problems. She had developed a nervous habit of looking over her shoulder, for something strange was going on in the Sesemann house. No matter how carefully the housekeeper checked the locks on the doors and windows each evening, in the

morning the big front door stood wide
open. How could that be?

One night, she persuaded
Sebastian and Johann the coachman to
sit up and watch the front door. The two
settled into a room off the front hall. As
the hours passed and nothing happened
their eyes grew heavy and soon the men
were asleep. Sometime during the night
a cold draft wakened Sebastian. He
jumped up and ran out into the hall.
The door stood wide open. He turned to
call Johann and an icy shiver ran up his
spine. On the stairway, something white
flickered for a moment—and was gone!

When Fräulein Rottenmeier heard about the figure in white, she wrote immediately to Herr Sesemann. Her fingers were numb with fright, she said, Herr Sesemann must come home immediately! Ghosts in the house might seriously damage his daughter's delicate health.

Herr Sesemann returned at once. "This is nonsense," he said, the minute he stepped into the front hall. "Ghost, indeed! Sebastian, how could a grown man be so foolish? I will sit up tonight and get to the bottom of this."

That evening, Herr Sesemann settled down with several candles and a book to wait for the ghost. His pocket watch was showing one o'clock when a sound caught his attention. Was that soft click a key turning in the lock? He edged cautiously into the hall. The front door stood open and the pale moonlight entered, lighting up a white form on the doorsill.

"Who is there?" Herr Sesemann thundered. The figure turned round with a little scream. It was Heidi, with bare feet, in her nightgown, looking confused and trembling like a leaf in the wind.

"Child, what does this mean?" demanded Herr Sesemann.

White with fright, Heidi whispered, "I don't know."

Moved by her confusion and fear, he said, more gently, "Come and sit down and tell me what the trouble is."

Herr Sesemann led Heidi into the small room beside the hall. Embers still burned in the fireplace and the room was warm, but Heidi shivered so much that her teeth chattered.

"Don't be afraid," Herr Sesemann said soothingly, wrapping a shawl around the girl. "Tell me where you were going."

"I was looking for the trees," Heidi began. "Every night when I close my eyes, I see the firs outside my window at my Grandfather's. The wind sings through the branches and I run outside to see the stars shining in the heavens. It is so beautiful. But when I open my eyes, it's gone. All I see are walls and streets. And I feel a great stone sitting on me, right here." Heidi lay her hand over her heart.

Herr Sesemann sighed and took her cold little hands into his large warm ones. "Come, I'll tuck you into bed."

At four-thirty the next morning, Herr Sesemann rapped loudly on the housekeeper's door. "Make haste, Fräulein," he called. "There is a journey to prepare for."

Then he went into his daughter's room and sat at the foot of her bed. "I know how much you love Heidi, Klara," he said. "But she is so homesick she walks in her sleep. I was shocked to see how ill she looks. We must think of her and not just ourselves, my dear."

Klara wiped a tear from her eye. "You're right, Papa. I mustn't be selfish. She should go home. Please ask Sebastian to bring Heidi's trunk to my room so that I may pack some surprises for her. Oh, and Papa, there's something else." Klara told her father the whole story about the white rolls, and he went off to tell Fräulein Rottenmeier to have a basket of fresh rolls packed immediately.

Heidi had no idea why Tinette had arrived in her room with orders to dress her in the best of Klara's hand-me-down dresses. She was even more puzzled to find a tearful Klara in the dining room. "How I shall miss you!" her friend cried.

Heidi looked around in amazement.

"You don't know anything about it," said Herr Sesemann, laughing. "Well, you are going home today, Heidi, right after breakfast."

"Home?" repeated Heidi. She could hardly catch her breath.

"Don't you want to know something about it?"

"Oh yes!" she cried.

"Well, then, so you shall. The carriage is being made ready to take you to the train. Sebastian will accompany you back to Dörfli. Now, eat a good breakfast and then go with Klara to pack your things."

Heidi was too excited to eat and Klara was already finished, so Sebastian wheeled Klara to her bedroom. In the middle of the floor stood a large trunk.

"Come see what I have packed for you," Klara called to her friend. The trunk held stacks of dresses and aprons, handkerchiefs, and sewing things. "And see here, Heidi," she added, holding up a basket of twelve soft white rolls. Heidi crowed with delight. Both girls had entirely forgotten that the moment had come for them to part. And when the call was heard—"The carriage is ready!"—there was no time left to be sad.

Heidi ran to her room to get her beautiful story book from its place beneath her pillow. She put it in the basket with the rolls. In her closet she found her old red shawl and her battered straw hat; Tinette had not thought them worth packing. Heidi wrapped the hat in the shawl and set the bundle on top of the basket. Then she put on a fine hat Klara had given her and left the room.

The two children had to say a speedy farewell, for the carriage was waiting. "I shall miss you so much!" Klara exclaimed. "But Papa has promised me that next spring we will come visit you in the mountains."

"Oh, Klara, you must come! The mountains will make you stronger, just the way they made me stronger."

Fräulein Rottenmeier interrupted their good-byes by taking the little red bundle out of Heidi's basket and throwing it on the floor.

"No, Adelheid, you cannot leave this house carrying a thing such as that," she said.

"Let the child take what she wishes," Herr Sesemann said sharply. "Now, my dear Heidi, here is a letter and a package for your grandfather—do not lose it. Sebastian will see you safely home."

Clutching the precious hat under one arm and the letter and package under the other, Heidi was lifted into the carriage.

"Good-bye!" called Klara.

"Pleasant journey!" her father added.

"Thank you!" Heidi called out the carriage window as Johann the coachman flicked his whip and they set off for the railway station.

Chapter

⑩

Home to the Alm

Two days later, Sebastian deposited Heidi's trunk and basket on the Maienfeld station platform. The train was whistling farther up the valley. Sebastian looked longingly after it, for he much preferred traveling in that safe and easy way to climbing a mountain on foot—a mountain which might be steep and dangerous besides.

Not far from the railway station

stood a little wagon, drawn by a lean horse; into this wagon a broad-shouldered man was loading several large bags which had been brought by the train. Sebastian stepped up to him and questioned him about the safest way to Dörfli.

"All ways are safe here," was the short reply. "If your trunk is not too heavy, I can take it up to the village—and the child as well."

"I can go alone," Heidi chimed in. "And I know the way from Dörfli up the Alm."

Sebastian knew that he ought to go with Heidi, but he agreed to let Heidi go alone. A heavy load was lifted from Sebastian's mind as he watched Heidi roll away on the cart's high seat. He hadn't had to climb a mountain after all. He sat down in the station to wait for the returning train.

The carter was curious about the child. "You must be the girl who used to live with the Alm Uncle. Didn't they treat you well down in the city?"

"They were very kind," Heidi replied.

"Then why didn't you stay?"

"Because I'd a thousand times rather be up on the mountain with Grandfather."

"Bah!" the man growled. "Perhaps you'll think differently when you get up there."

'But I wonder,' he thought to himself, 'if she knows how it is.'

When the cart reached Dörfli, Heidi grabbed her basket and started up the path. "Thank you. Grandfather will come for the trunk," she called back.

So the carter was left to pass on to the villagers the surprising news that Heidi had returned to the Alm Uncle.

Heidi ran as fast as she could up the mountain, with one thought in her mind, 'Will the grandmother be sitting by her spinning wheel? Or has she died since I've been gone?'

Now she had reached the hollow where the grandmother's hut stood, and her heart began to throb. She could hardly open the door, she trembled so. She ran to the middle of the room and stood there, too out of breath to speak.

"Heavens!" sounded from the corner, "our Heidi used to run in like that! Who has come in?"

Rushing into the corner and into the grandmother's lap, the girl was unable to say anything more from sheer delight.

"Dear child, you're back! Thank heavens!"

"And I'll never leave again," Heidi promised. "Here's a present for you." She pressed one of the rolls into Grannie's hands. "Now you won't have to eat that hard, black bread."

Just then Brigitte appeared in the doorway, "Heidi!" she gasped. "I can't believe my eyes. Oh, Mother, if you

could see the beautiful dress she's wearing. And a hat with a feather. Why, I hardly recognized her!"

"I must go home to my grandfather," said Heidi, "but tomorrow I will come to you again; good night, Grandmother."

"Yes, come again, Heidi," said the old woman, and she pressed Heidi's hand between her own and could hardly let go.

"Why have you taken off your beautiful dress?" asked Brigitte.

"Because grandfather might not know me if I went to him in it."

"He will know you; but you must be careful. Peter says the Alm Uncle has become very cross."

But Heidi was already running up the footpath. Several times she paused to catch her breath and to gaze at the mountain peaks blazing red in the setting sun. By the time she reached the hut, where her grandfather sat smoking

his pipe, she was panting so hard that all she could do was drop her basket and fall into her grandfather's arms.

"So you have come home again, Heidi. Did they send you away?"

"Oh no, Grandfather," Heidi answered. "They were all so good to me. But I could hardly bear being away from home; I often thought I would smother, it choked me so. Then one morning Herr Sesemann called me very early and said I was going home. Perhaps it tells all about it in his letter"—and she took the letter and the package from her basket and laid it on the old man's knee.

After he had read the letter he handed her the package. "This belongs to you. It is enough money to buy a bed and clothes."

"I don't need it, Grandfather," said Heidi. "I have a bed, and Klara gave me so many clothes I shall never need any more."

"Take it and put it in the cupboard; you will use it someday."

Heidi obeyed and skipped into the hut where she was delighted to see everything again. She climbed the ladder to the loft, but—"Grandfather," she cried, "I no longer have a bed!"

"You will soon have another," he replied. "I didn't know you would return; now come and get your milk."

Heidi came down and took her seat on the high stool. She drank the goat's milk as eagerly as if she had never had anything so precious in her reach before.

A shrill whistle sounded outside. Heidi shot out the door like lightning. There was Peter and his flock of goats.

"So you're back," Peter cried. "Will you come with me to the pasture tomorrow?"

"Not tomorrow," said Heidi, as she kissed Little Swan and Little Bear. "I promised to visit your grandmother tomorrow. But soon."

Heidi led the two little goats off to

their stalls, then returned to the hut to find the old man tucking her sheet around a new bed of fresh-smelling hay. Heidi lay down, gave a great yawn, and in no time at all she was asleep. During the night, her grandfather left his couch at least ten times, climbing the ladder to see if Heidi was truly home with him again.

The next day, the Alm Uncle took Heidi to visit Peter's grandmother while he set off down the mountain to fetch Heidi's trunk.

"Ah, child," the old woman cried, "the roll was so tasty, so soft. I feel stronger already!"

"But you must eat more than one, Grandmother."

"Mother wants to make them last as long as possible," Brigitte explained.

"But they'll grow stale!"

Then Heidi remembered the package she'd carried home from Frankfurt. "I have lots of money," she said. "Peter shall take some to the village baker and buy you a fresh roll every day."

"Oh, no, child—" Brigitte began.

"Yes," Heidi insisted. "Now, then, Grandmother, shall I read to you?"

Both women gasped. "Can you read, Heidi?"

Heidi climbed on a chair and brought down the hymnbook. "What would you like to hear?"

"Anything you like, child," said the old woman eagerly.

"Here is something about the sun; I will read it for you:

"Today we languish
In grief and anguish,
But earthly sorrow
Shall fade tomorrow:
After the storm the sun shines
bright.

Sweet peace and pleasure
In boundless measure
We know is given
In the gardens of heaven;
And thither my hopes yearn
day and night!"

"Oh Heidi, that gives me light! It gives me light in my heart. Oh, how much good you have done me, Heidi!" the old woman exclaimed, her face jubilant with happiness.

Chapter

(11)

Another Visitor

During the long snowy winter, Klara wrote many letters to Heidi promising to visit in the spring. At first it seemed to Heidi as if the spring would never come, but after the Alm Uncle rented a little house in Dörfli so that Heidi could attend the village school, the time passed quickly.

Heidi was a good student and was soon at the head of the class, but her friend Peter paid no attention to his lessons.

"You are going to learn to read," she told him. So, with her help, and despite his grumbling, Peter was soon reciting his ABC's. By the end of the winter, he could even read some of the simpler hymns to his grandmother.

May had come again. From every height the overflowing brooks rushed down into the valley. The spring wind blew through the fir trees and shook off the old, dark needles so the young, green ones could dress the trees in beauty.

Heidi ran here and there and could not tell which spot was the loveliest. It seemed as if all creatures were singing with delight: "On the Alm! On the Alm!"

Heidi, her grandfather, and the goats moved back to the hut on the Alm. From the workshop behind the house came the sound of busy hammering and sawing. In front of the workshop door there stood a fine new stool, and her grandfather was working on another.

"Oh, I know what that is for!" exclaimed Heidi. "That will be needed when Klara comes from Frankfurt! There will have to be one for her grandmamma, and another for Fräulein Rottenmeier."

"I don't know if the fräulein will be coming or not," said the grandfather,

"but it will be safer to have one ready, so that we can invite her to sit down if she comes."

Heidi looked at the little wooden stool. "I don't believe she would sit on it," she said doubtfully.

"Then we will invite her to the sofa with the beautiful green grass covering," he replied, gesturing toward the yard.

Suddenly, there came the whistling sound of a rod swinging through the air. Heidi ran out of the woodshed and was surrounded in a twinkling by the leaping goats. Peter pushed them all away, for he had a letter to give Heidi.

"It's from Klara! 'Everything is packed,'" she read aloud. "'I can hardly wait to see you.'"

Peter turned away scowling as he drove the frightened goats up the mountain. He didn't want to share Heidi with anybody—particularly not the people who had taken her away to Frankfurt.

On the day Klara was expected,

Heidi sat out on the grandfather's bench watching for the visitors. Soon she saw an odd procession winding its way up the mountain. First came two men carrying Klara in a sedan chair, then a man with Klara's wheelchair upended on his head, then two with great baskets strapped to their backs. Bringing up the rear was a man leading a white pony ridden by Frau Sesemann.

"There they are! There they are!" screamed Heidi, jumping up in the air with delight.

"My dear Alm Uncle," the old woman called in her friendly way, "what a fine view you have! Many a king might envy you! And how well Heidi looks—like a June rose."

The men put the chair down on the ground, and Heidi and Klara greeted each other joyfully.

"Oh how beautiful it is here!" Klara said. The grandfather lifted her gently from the sedan into her wheelchair and

Heidi pushed her so that she could see the goat shed and the singing fir trees and the flower-strewn meadow. Soon they were sitting at the table that the Alm Uncle had placed outside.

"Klara," Frau Sesemann exclaimed halfway through the meal of bread and

toasted cheese. "I have never seen you eat so much."

"Everything tastes so much better here than in Frankfurt. I don't think I've ever been so hungry!" the girl replied.

The grandfather turned to the grandmamma. "If you would allow it, we

would like for Klara to stay here with us for the summer. The mountain air would be good for her."

"My dear Uncle," the old lady said, a twinkle in her eye. "You have read my mind."

The two girls shouted with joy like two escaped birds, and the grandmamma's face lit up with sunshine.

When the hired men came toiling up the mountain again with the sedan chair and the white pony, only Frau Sesemann returned with them. The Alm

Uncle himself took the bridle and led the pony down the steep mountain.

Of all the wonders of that marvelous day, the best for Klara was snuggling into the bed the grandfather had made for her in the loft and looking through the round window at the starry sky.

"Oh, Heidi," she breathed, "being up here is like riding through the heavens."

The weeks passed happily for the two girls. Every morning the grandfather

carried Klara down the ladder to her wheelchair. Heidi pushed her along the rocky path so they could collect blue-bells and blue gentians. Often they sat and talked, or wrote letters to the grand-mamma. Every morning and every evening Peter came by with the goats. Klara soon learned their names and longed to play with them, but Peter always brandished his stick furiously and drove the goats past the hut as quickly as he could.

One morning, however, the Alm Uncle called Peter aside.

"From today on let Little Swan do as he likes," he said. "She knows where the sweetest herbs and grasses are, so that she will give splendid milk. If she climbs high up on the mountain peaks, follow her, understand? Why are you looking as if you would like to swallow someone, Peter? No one is in your way. Now go!"

Peter was accustomed to following the Alm Uncle's orders, and he set off

with his goats obediently. A sudden thought, however, made him call out to Heidi who was leaping alongside the flock as they bounded up the path. "You must come with me," he said harshly.

"No," she replied. "I cannot come to the pasture so long as Klara is with us."

With that, she tore herself away from the goats and ran back inside the hut. Peter was so angry he shook both fists at the empty wheelchair that stood innocently beside the doorway. Then he ran up the mountain with his flock springing along behind him.

Chapter

12

Something Unexpected Happens

"How I wish I could go up the mountain with Peter," Klara told Heidi and the Alm Uncle as they sat at the breakfast table. "I would love to see the high meadow."

"Klara is now drinking two bowls of Little Swan's milk at each meal, just as I do," Heidi said. "Do you think she is strong enough to go to the high pasture and spend a day with the goats?"

The grandfather stroked his beard thoughtfully. "You do look stronger, child. Will you try, just once, to stand on the ground?"

Klara looked frightened. "It will hurt," she said.

"I will hold you. Try just for a moment."

Because she wanted to please him, Klara gritted her teeth and, clutching the old man's arm, pulled herself up from her chair and stood on trembling legs.

"Wonderful!" the grandfather said, easing her back into the chair. "We'll try it."

The next morning they were having their breakfast when Peter arrived with the goats. He did not give his customary whistle, and his flock were not milling around him as trustingly as usual; Peter had been striking them with his stick. His anger had reached the boiling point. Again he glowered at the wheelchair standing by the door. It seemed to Peter like an enemy.

Peter looked around him; everything was still. On impulse, he rushed at the chair and gave it a mighty push. It began rolling crazily toward the slope of the mountain, and in a moment it had disappeared over the edge. Then Peter rushed up the Alm as if he had wings.

"Where is the chair?" Heidi asked when the grandfather carried Klara outside. She looked all around the hut. "Could the wind have blown it down the slope?"

"And where is Peter?" inquired the old man. "Our goats are still in the shed."

"What shall I do without my chair?" Klara cried. "I shall never get to see the high alp!"

"I'll carry you up," the grandfather replied.

When they reached the high meadow, they found the herd grazing peacefully, but Peter was nowhere to be seen. Heidi soon noticed him crouching behind a large rock.

"What's wrong with him, Grandfather? He acts just like a goat who expects a beating."

"Perhaps," the grandfather said dryly as he settled Klara on a blanket on the ground, "he deserves a beating."

With that, the grandfather left them a packed lunch and went back down the mountain path. He would return in the evening.

Heidi began picking flowers in a nearby meadow to make a bouquet for Klara. "If only you could see the bluebells nodding in the sunlight, Klara," she called. "I can almost hear their bells ringing."

Heidi returned to her friend's side for a moment, then suggested, "The meadow is only a few steps up the mountain, around those rocks. If I held you, perhaps you could walk that far."

"Oh, no! You're much too small to hold me up."

"I'll ask Peter to help."

Heidi ran up the mountain to where Peter lay staring sulkily into the distance. "Come help me, Peter."

"No!" he said, refusing to look at her.

Suddenly fed up with Peter's bad moods, Heidi stamped her foot and shouted, "You'd better come and help or you'll be sorry!"

Peter looked up in alarm. Did she

know about the wheelchair? Would she tell the Alm Uncle? Although Heidi had only meant that she wouldn't give him an extra helping of cheese at lunch, Peter's guilty conscience made him leap up and follow her.

Between the two of them, they soon had Klara on her feet and struggling up the slope. It hurt more than Klara would let on. She had tears in her eyes and was breathing heavily. She tried to bear her weight on her feet a little, but she could not move them forward.

"Just stamp down hard," suggested Heidi, "then it will hurt you less afterwards."

Klara tried taking one firm step on the ground and then another; but it hurt so much she gave a little scream. Still, she took another step.

"That didn't hurt nearly so much," she said.

"Do it once more," urged Heidi eagerly.

Klara did so, then again and again, crying out, "I can, Heidi! Oh, I can! See! See! I can take steps, one after another."

"Oh, oh!" shouted Heidi. "Now you can walk!"

When they reached the meadow, they all collapsed onto the soft grass.

"Oh how beautiful!" Klara sighed. "How glad I am that I could come here."

That evening, the grandfather came for the girls and carried Klara back to the hut. She slept more soundly than ever before, and in the morning, she tried again to walk. As the days passed, her trembling steps grew more and more sure. When a letter arrived to say that Frau Sesemann would be arriving soon, Klara decided to keep her wonderful news a surprise.

Chapter

13

Miracle on the Mountain

The morning the visitor was expected, Heidi and Klara sat out on the grandfather's bench looking down over the valley. At last they saw the grandmamma, on her white pony.

When Frau Sesemann was near enough, she called out, "Klara, why aren't you in your chair?"

Alarmed, the grandmamma dismounted hastily. "But Klara," she cried, as she approached the hut, "Is it really you, so red-cheeked and round as an apple? Child! I hardly know you!"

With that, Heidi slipped her arm under Klara's, and the two girls stood and began to walk towards the visitor. Frau Sesemann stood still, at first from fear, but then from surprise as she realized that Klara was walking upright.

The grandmamma began to laugh and cry at once, and touched Klara's arm just to be sure that what she saw was real. She rushed to the Alm Uncle and grasped both of his hands.

"My dear Uncle! My dear Uncle! How much my son and I have to thank you for!"

"No, no," he said. "It was the sunshine and mountain air that made her better."

"And Little Swan's lovely milk, too," added Klara.

Just then, Peter's whistle sounded and he and the goats came bounding down the mountain. The grandmamma was enchanted to see the animals she had heard so much about.

"Come here, my boy," she called to Peter.

Stricken with terror and guilt, Peter stared at the well-dressed old woman and began babbling, "I'm sorry! I didn't mean to, and now it's all smashed to pieces."

Frau Sesemann turned with puzzled eyes to the Alm Uncle. "What is wrong with the boy?"

"I imagine," he said, "that Peter is speaking of Klara's wheelchair. He is the wind that blew it down the mountain. And now he fears he will be punished."

The grandmamma looked into Peter's terrified face and said, "No, my dear Uncle. The boy has been punished enough. But here is something to think about, boy. Anyone who does a wrong deed and thinks no one sees it is mistaken. This time wickedness was turned to good, for Klara tried even harder to walk once she lost her chair. But you must remember always to think before you are tempted to do a wicked act. Do you understand?"

Peter nodded.

"Good," the grandmamma said, and smiled. "Now I should like to give you a present to remember the people from Frankfurt. What would you like to have most in the world?"

Peter could hardly believe his ears. A present rather than a whipping? "A penny," he said.

The old woman smiled and took a dollar from her purse.

"Here we have a hundred pennies. Two for every week of the year." Then she called Heidi to stand by her side. "And you, dear child," she said. "What would you like?"

Heidi didn't need to think. She knew just what she wanted.

"The bed I had in Frankfurt for Peter's grandmother, so she'll never have to sleep in a cold, hard bed again."

"Dear child," the grandmother said, kissing her, "it shall be sent as soon as I return to Frankfurt."

Klara spent one last night in the loft bedroom under the stars. The next

morning, when it was time for the Alm Uncle to carry her down the mountain to the waiting carriage that would take her home, Klara shed hot tears because she had to leave the beautiful Alm.

Heidi comforted her and said, "It will be summer again in no time, and then you will come back, and it will be more beautiful than ever. You will walk everywhere, and we can go up to the pasture with the goats every day and be jolly."

"I will leave a greeting for Peter," Klara said through her tears, "and for the goats. I would like to send Little Swan a present so she won't forget me."

"That's easy," Heidi replied. "Send her a little salt. You know how gladly she licks the salt from grandfather's hand at night."

"Oh, then I will certainly send her a hundred pounds of salt from Frankfurt!" Klara laughed.

Then the grandmother and Klara mounted their ponies—for Klara was now able to ride down and no longer

needed a sedan chair. Heidi stationed herself at the farthest edge of the slope and waved her hand to Klara and the grandmamma until the last speck of horse and rider had disappeared. "Summer will come again!" she called to her cherished friends.

And so it did.

THE END

ABOUT THE AUTHOR

Johanna Heusser grew up in the early 1800s in the little Swiss village of Hirzel. The beautiful countryside and majestic mountains she loved as a child set the backdrop for *Heidi*, her first book, published in 1881.

Like the character of Heidi, the author's formal education was not very successful. She left the village school and was sent to study with the pastor of her church. She later married Bernhard Spyri, and they had a son.

Johanna Spyri's love of nature and extraordinary kindness inspired all who knew her. She wrote *Heidi* in an effort to raise money for war relief.

Unfortunately, both her husband and son died before her. She continued to write stories for children until her death in 1901.

The Young Collector's
Illustrated Classics

The Adventures of Robin Hood
The Adventures of Tom Sawyer
Black Beauty
Call of the Wild
Dracula
Frankenstein
Gulliver's Travels
Heidi
Hunchback of Notre Dame
Little Women
Moby Dick
Oliver Twist
Peter Pan
The Prince and the Pauper
The Secret Garden
The Strange Case of Dr. Jekyll & Mr. Hyde
Swiss Family Robinson
Treasure Island
20,000 Leagues Under the Sea
White Fang

Masterwork Classics are available for special
and educational sales from:

Kidsbooks, Inc.
3535 West Peterson Avenue
Chicago, IL 60659
(312) 509-0707